W9-DFQ-293

ISLAND ROSE
by L.E. Williams

Illustrations by
Tony Meers

Spot Illustrations by
Catherine Huerta

MAGIC ATTIC PRESS

Published by Magic Attic Press.

This book is dedicated to a fellow beach lover—Maryellen Duffy

For more information contact:
Book Editor, Magic Attic Press, 866 Spring Street,
Westbrook, ME 04092-3808

First Edition
Printed in the United States of America
1 2 3 4 5 6 7 8 9 10

Magic Attic Club® is a registered trademark.

Betsy Gould, Publisher
Marva Martin, Art Director
Jay Brady, Managing Editor

Edited by Judit Bodnar
Designed by Cindy Vacek

Williams,L.E.
Island Rose / by L.E. Williams:
illustrations by Tony Meers, spot illustrations by Catherine Huerta.
(Magic Attic Club)
Summary: Rose finds herself on a tropical island. She has entered a surfing contest and
Haku is determined to beat Rose and win the contest. But when Haku catches a wave and
disappears no one else seems to notice. Can Rose save him and risk losing the contest?
ISBN 1-57513-126-9 (hardback) ISBN 1-57513-125-0 (paperback)
ISBN 1-57513-145-5 (library edition hardback)

Library of Congress Cataloging in Publication Data is on file at the Library of Congress

As members of the
MAGIC ATTIC CLUB,
we promise to
be best friends,
share all of our adventures in the attic,
use our imaginations,
have lots of fun together,
and remember—the real magic is in us.

Alison   *Keisha*

Heather   *Megan*

Rose

Table of Contents

Island Rose
Prologue

When Alison, Heather, Keisha, and Megan find a golden key buried in the snow, they have no idea that it will change their lives forever. They discover that it belongs to Ellie Goodwin, the owner of an old Victorian house across the street from Alison's. Ellie, grateful when they return the key to her, invites the girls to play in her attic. There they find a steamer trunk filled with wonderful outfits—party dresses, a princess gown, a ballet tutu, cowgirl clothes, and many, many, more. The girls try on some of the costumes and admire their reflections in a tall, gilded mirror nearby. Suddenly they are transported to a new time and place, embarking on the greatest adventure of their lives.

After they return to the present and Ellie's attic, they form the Magic Attic Club, promising to tell each other every exciting detail of their future adventures. Then they meet Rose Hopkins, a new girl at school, and invite her to join the club and share their amazing secret.

Chapter
One

A NEW JOB

Ellie Goodwin clasped her hands together, her bright blue eyes shining. "Oh, Rose, you're a genius."

Rose Hopkins smiled as she gazed at the computer screen. She liked being called a genius. During the past week, she had been teaching her neighbor how to use a new gardening program. Ellie's garden was all laid out on the screen, in plenty of time for spring planting.

Rose clicked the mouse on the Print icon. "Now you'll know exactly what seeds to order, and how many," she explained.

Ellie patted Rose on the back as the color printer started to work. "I love how the program tells you what plants to put near each other," she said. "I never knew that asparagus and tomatoes thrive when they're planted side by side. I've never had much luck with asparagus."

"You will this summer," Rose said confidently. "Mr. Aust at the computer store said this is the best program out there. And he should know—he's a gardener, too."

The printer stopped whirring, and Ellie picked up the garden plan. "Now I'm going to pore over the seed catalogs I've been collecting and get my orders in the mail before it's too late."

Rose stood up. "And I have to go home and get my homework finished."

A New Job

Ellie walked Rose through the high-ceilinged foyer to the front door. "Thank you so much for your help," she said to her young friend.

"No problem," Rose said with a wave of her hand.

Ellie paused, her hand on the doorknob. "You know," she said slowly, "since you love the computer so much, I have an idea. I give a young boy voice lessons. His mother mentioned he needs a little tutoring on using Windows." Then she shook her head. "Oh, never mind. You're much too busy to take on another task."

"I could do it," Rose protested. A feeling of satisfaction warmed her. It felt good to know Ellie thought so highly of her computer skills. "I'd be more than happy to."

Ellie's brow wrinkled. "Are you sure, dear? I hate to burden you."

"He's just a kid, right?"

"Blake Muller is eight. He's very bright. I'm sure he'd catch on quickly with a good teacher such as you."

Rose grinned. "No problem."

Ellie opened the door. "You're a lifesaver. I'll have

Blake's mother give you a call. She's at her wit's end trying to find another teacher. So far three of them have quit."

Rose stopped on the porch, suddenly uneasy, and turned to look at Ellie. "He's already had three computer teachers? Why did they all quit?"

Ellie shrugged. "Mrs. Muller didn't tell me."

"Oh." Rose pondered that a moment, but she couldn't think of anything to say. It was too late now anyway; she had already agreed. Besides, she could handle an eight-year-old. She waved to Ellie and trotted home. Her parents wouldn't be there yet, but she couldn't wait to tell her grandfather about her new job.

Rose wiped her sweaty palms on her jeans as she waited for Blake to come downstairs. Mrs. Muller said he was practicing a solo for his lesson with Ellie.

Why was she so nervous? He's just a kid, she kept telling herself. She didn't want to mess up, not with Ellie recommending her for this job and all.

The loud ticking of the wall clock was driving Rose crazy as she waited and waited. Slowly she became less nervous and more frustrated. She hated waiting.

Finally, she heard footsteps clumping down the stairs.

A boy with short blond hair and a round face burst into the room and launched himself into the chair in front of the computer. He was wearing slacks and a maroon sweater. "Hi, I'm Blake. Sorry I'm late, but I had to memorize the last lines for a song I'm learning."

Rose lifted her eyebrows. "Really? That's interesting."

The boy leaned back in his chair and smiled as though he were giving an interview for a television show. "Yes, it's very interesting. It's a song from *The Sound of Music*. You probably don't know it."

"Actually," Rose said, "I do know that musical. It's one of my favorites."

For a second, Blake looked surprised. "Well, I'm sure you don't know the words to the song 'Edelweiss.'"

"You're right about that. But since I'm only here for half an hour and we're getting started a bit late, let's get on the computer, okay?"

Blake shrugged. "Sure."

"You know this is your mouse, right?" Rose asked, pointing to the egg-shaped object next to the computer.

Blake nodded, looking at the clock.

"Well, using Windows is very easy. All you have to do is point and click." Rose looked at her student. He was tapping his fingers against the keyboard as though it were a drum set. "Are you listening?" she asked him.

The tapping stopped. "Huh?"

"I guess not," Rose said, wondering if this was such a great idea after all. "Pay attention or you won't learn anything."

Blake frowned. "Who cares about the dumb old computer anyway? I told my mom I don't want to learn. I'd rather sing. Do you want to hear me sing? I could sing to you in French, or even German."

Rose stopped herself from rolling her eyes. "We only have fifteen minutes left. Why don't you try using the mouse?"

Blake put his hand on the mouse and clicked it all over the screen. Nothing happened. "See? Computers are stupid. Did Ellie tell you I'm her best singer?"

"The mouse didn't work because you have to put the arrow on something and then click or double-click," Rose said, putting her hand over his and guiding it toward one of the shortcut icons.

"I've been taking lessons for five years," the boy announced.

Rose pulled her hand away in surprise. "Computer lessons?"

Blake scowled. "Are you kidding? Voice lessons, of course. Ellie is the best teacher I've ever had. She says I'll be performing on Broadway in New York City someday."

Rose sighed, her shoulders drooping. Now she knew why three computer teachers had quit. Then she sat up straighter in her chair. She was determined not to be the fourth. She'd stick it out, no matter what.

"Want to hear me do my scales?" Blake asked, tossing the mouse from hand to hand.

Rose gritted her teeth. No matter what, she reminded herself.

Chapter
Two

WHAT TO DO?

Rose walked over to Alison McCann's house. She had just finished her fourth lesson with Blake in three weeks, and if she didn't talk to her best friends right away, she would scream.

She found the girls upstairs, in Alison's room.

"Here's the computer whiz," Keisha Vance teased as Rose flopped on the floor with a deep moan of disgust.

Megan Rider tossed a pillow in Rose's direction. "How did the lesson go today? Did Bratty Blake behave?"

Rose took the pillow, which had bounced off her stomach, and tucked it under her head. It was her friends who had come up with the name Bratty Blake. He wasn't really a brat, he was just—impossible!

"I got nothing accomplished today, as usual," Rose said." All he wants to do is talk about how great he is. If I have to listen to any more from Blake Muller, I just might have to give up computers forever."

"Well, maybe he *is* great, and you should listen to him," Heather Hardin said, looking serious.

All the girls stared at her in stunned silence.

A moment later, Heather cracked a smile. "Gotcha!" she shouted.

The girls laughed, and Rose breathed a sigh of relief. For a moment she had thought Heather was for real. "What should I do about him?" she asked. "He's driving me crazy."

Alison was lolling on her bed. She said "I know! Just

fake being sick."

Rose shook her head. "That'll only work for one week. I can't be sick every Thursday."

"I have a better idea," Keisha said. She was sitting on the floor, doing leg stretches. "Tell Blake's mother you have a school project to do and you can only work on it on Thursdays."

"What if she wants to change the day of the lesson?" Alison said.

"Never mind," Rose said. "I can't lie like that anyway."

Megan waved her hand in the air. "My turn. Tell Bratty Blake that you're sick of hearing him talk about himself and that he's totally boring, so he should just stop it."

"At least you wouldn't be lying," Alison said with a giggle.

"That wouldn't be very nice," Heather said from her perch on a rocking chair in a corner of the room. "I think you should tell Ellie your problem. Maybe she'll have a suggestion for you. After all, she gives him lessons, too."

Rose sat up. "I guess I could do that."

"That's a great idea," Keisha said. Alison and Megan
nodded in agreement.

"Yikes!" said Megan, looking at her watch. "Sorry, guys,
but I have to get going. I promised my aunt I'd be home
in time to help with supper."

"I'd better go, too," Heather said. "I have tons of
homework."

"Are you leaving, too, Keisha?" Rose asked.

"Alison and I are going to do that monster math
assignment together. Do you want to stay and help?"

Rose hesitated. She wasn't sure she could concentrate
on homework.

"Come on, Rose," said Heather, "we'll walk you across
the street to Ellie's. The sooner you solve this problem,
the sooner you'll feel better about it."

"You're right." Rose stood up. "I knew I could count on
you guys for help." She flipped her ponytail over her
shoulder and followed Heather and Megan out of the room.

"Let us know what happens right away," Keisha called
after her.

"I will," Rose called back.

When she reached Ellie's walkway, she waved good-bye to her friends. It felt great to finally be doing something about her problem rather than just complaining about it. She hadn't even told her family about her frustrations teaching Blake the computer—or rather, not teaching him. She didn't think he'd learned one thing in the four lessons so far. He still didn't even know how to point and click with the mouse. She, on the other hand, knew his whole life's story.

Rose ran up the steps and rang the doorbell. She heard music from inside. Suddenly it stopped.

A moment later, Ellie opened the door. "Come in, come in," she said to Rose with a big smile. "I thought you might be the mail carrier bringing my seed orders."

Rose stepped into the foyer. "Are you giving a lesson?"

"I am, but if you wait for ten minutes, I'll be through."

Rose tried to hide her disappointment. She hated to wait even ten more minutes to get Ellie's advice. "Okay," she agreed.

"In fact," Ellie went on, closing the door against the cool spring air, "it's Blake Muller having his voice lesson. Would you like to come listen?"

Rose swallowed a groan. That was the last thing she wanted to do. But instead of saying what she was thinking—"Absolutely no way!"—she shook her head politely. "If you don't mind, maybe I'll just check out the attic?"

"Why certainly, my dear." Ellie gently took Rose by the shoulders and turned her in the direction of the silver box that held the special key. "When the lesson is over, we'll sit and chat."

Rose nodded. "I'd like that."

With a smile, Ellie disappeared behind the mahogany doors of the music room. Rose took the golden key and practically ran up the two flights to the attic.

Chapter Three

ISLAND ROSE

A t the top of the stairs, Rose pulled the cord to turn on the overhead attic light. In the rosy glow, she headed right for the open trunk. Kneeling on the thick oriental rug, she stuck her hands in the mounds of material inside it. She loved the feel of the different fabrics—the smooth silks and satins, the soft velvets, scratchy wools, and even the bumpy beads.

Looking at the costumes in the trunk was always exciting. It seemed as though there were new clothes in there every time Rose opened it. She loved trying to guess what kind of adventure she might have in each outfit. When she put on a costume and looked in Ellie's mirror, she never knew where she'd end up.

Rose wiggled her fingers through the heavy folds of cloth, gently moving aside the layers. The faint tinkling of the piano came through the floorboards, and she could just picture the "Aren't I wonderful?" look on Blake's face. She tried to block out the sound. The last thing she wanted to do was think about that boy having his voice lesson downstairs. He was the whole reason she was so upset.

She shook her head, trying to get her mind off Blake, and caught a glimpse of green straw in the trunk. Puzzled, she grabbed a clump of it and gently pulled. No, it wasn't straw; it was a grass skirt.

With a broad smile, Rose stood up and held the skirt to her waist, moving her hips from side to side as though she were doing a Tahitian or Hawaiian dance. She pictured a tropical island like the one on the postcard her uncle had sent her last year. Wouldn't it be wonderful to live on an exotic island where there were no worries—and no computer lessons!

Rose quickly changed into a brightly flowered pair of shorts and top she found in the trunk, then tied the grass skirt on over that. She kicked off her sneakers and socks, then placed a beautiful flower in her hair.

Taking a deep breath, she tiptoed to the mirror. When she saw herself, she burst out laughing with delight. With her dark hair, she looked like an island girl. All she needed was a flower lei to complete the picture.

Her head swam with dizziness, and the next thing she knew she felt the hot sun shining down on her. Crowds of people were swarming in all directions, calling to one another and laughing, occasionally jostling her as they passed. And the air smelled like flowers and food from the many stands lining the street.

A hand grabbed Rose's arm.

"Come on," a girl said, pulling her along. "Don't just stand there. Let's look around."

Rose stared at the girl. She was about Rose's height, and she also had long dark hair. Around her head she wore a wreath of flowers.

The girl turned to her with a smile. "Isn't this fun? This has always been my favorite festival."

Rose nodded, wondering where the mirror had taken her.

The girl stopped in front of a booth. On the counter a velvet cloth had been spread out. Rose gasped when she saw what covered the cloth—pearls. Giant pearls, small pearls, all different colors, from black to pale pink.

"Oooh," Rose said admiringly, leaning forward to look at an especially large silver one.

The girl beside her sighed, too. "That one is my favorite," she said as she pointed to a blue pearl that wasn't completely round. In fact, it looked like a heart.

The woman behind the counter smiled at them. "Have

you saved your money, Leila, for one of my famous island
pearls?" she asked.

Rose silently thanked the woman for letting her know
the girl's name. Looking around at the palm trees and the
glittering ocean in the distance, she guessed they were
on some tropical island.

Leila shook her head. "I keep spending it on candy
and books."

The woman laughed. "And how about you, Rose? Which one do you like?"

"All of them," Rose admitted. "They're all beautiful."

"Yes, they are," the woman said, nodding. "And very precious." She waved her hands. "Now get on your way, girls, and let someone with real money look at my pearls." Then she winked at them.

Giggling, the girls moved on to the next booth, where they admired the jewelry. Rose especially liked a delicate shell necklace with a small sand dollar hanging from the center.

"Let's get something to eat," Leila said. "Do you want chocolate croissants or coconut ice cream?"

Rose thought a moment. Croissants, she knew, were a French-style roll. She remembered reading somewhere that a lot of the islands in the South Pacific belonged to France. But with the hot sun, something cold and sweet sounded perfect.

"Ice cream," she finally said.

Leila laughed. "Me, too." She hooked arms with Rose.

As they walked down the crowded streets to find an ice cream stand, Rose noticed a young boy trailing behind them. Whenever she turned to look at him, he was staring pointedly at anything but her and Leila. But when she turned away, she was sure she felt him watching them.

Oh, come on, Rose, she told herself, he's probably just some kid playing spy or something.

Leila tugged at her arm. "You did so great in the dance contest. Too bad you didn't win. You deserved to."

"Uh, thanks," Rose said, hoping she wasn't scheduled for a rematch. She didn't know the first thing about dancing island style.

"But I just know you'll win the surfing contest," Leila added confidently. "You're the best."

Rose gulped. Surfing? As in big waves? No way! She couldn't get on a board and try to outrun a bunch of waves. The ocean was way too scary!

31

"Everyone says you're going to win," Leila continued.

"She is not," a voice piped up. "I'm going to win."

Rose turned to look at the speaker. It was the boy who had been following them.

Leila laughed. "You think you are going to win, Haku? Maybe in your dreams."

The boy scowled as he looked up at them. He jammed his fists against his hips and spread his feet. "I've been practicing a lot. I could win. Just you wait and see."

"I'm sure you'll be wonderful," Rose said with a smile.

Leila shook her head. "You'll be one of the youngest kids in the contest, but Rose will be one of the oldest, and the best."

"You're just saying that because she's your friend," Haku said, sticking out his lower lip. "Wait till you see me out there. Papa says I'm the very best surfer he's ever seen."

Haku glowered as he turned to Rose. "I'll be better than you. I've been practicing every day. You watch. I'll beat you, Rose. I'll win the trophy."

"We'll see," Rose said.

"Little brothers!" Leila said in an exasperated tone. "Just ignore him, Rose."

While they had talked about the surfing contest, the crowd had grown even larger, surging around them.

"I wonder where everyone is going," said Rose.

"Just go with the flow," Leila answered, "and we'll know pretty soon. Come on, Haku."

At last the rush of people stopped.

"What's going on?" Haku asked, jumping up and down, trying to see over the heads of the adults standing around them.

"It must be a festival demonstration," Leila replied.

Rose smiled at Haku's excitement. "Want me to hold you up?"

"No, thanks," he said.

"Come on, then." She grabbed his hand and squeezed ahead through the crush of people.

Chapter

Four

HIDE–AND–SEEK

R ose nudged Haku to the front of the crowd so he had a clear view. Next to them a woman was kneeling on the ground, smashing something in a large, stone mortar with a stone pestle. She wore a piece of brown and tan patterned cloth wrapped around her like a towel, and flowers adorned her hair. Shell necklaces, bracelets, and anklets jangled with each movement.

An announcer explained that the woman was demonstrating pounding taro root into poi.

A couple of young girls offered the crowd bits of taro on a banana leaf. Rose took a small square of the gray-brown root and dipped it in the pile of sugar next to it. She popped it into her mouth.

Haku made a face at her. "That's yucky," he said.

Rose chewed on the taro. It had the consistency of a sweet potato, but it didn't have much flavor, though the sugar helped.

Next, poi was offered in a wooden bowl. Rose watched the man next to her dip two fingers into the pasty-looking mush, then lick it off his fingers. It didn't look very appetizing, but she was determined to try it. She dipped her fingers into the mush and tentatively licked it off. Not only did it look like muddy glue, but it tasted like it and felt like it in her mouth.

"Now *that* was yucky," she exclaimed.

Leila and Haku laughed at her expression.

"Come on," Leila said, "we're running out of time. Let's

change into our bathing suits first. Then we'll get our ice cream, and maybe something else, too. You'll need strength to catch those waves."

Rose tried to ignore her wobbling legs. How hard could it be to surf? All she had to do was stand up on a board and balance, right?

Leila led Rose and Haku to a cabana. Inside, there were lockers and doors to women's and men's dressing rooms. She opened a locker and handed her brother his swim trunks. They were bright orange and purple and looked like they'd hang down to his knees.

Leila grabbed her suit and handed one to Rose. "We'll meet you out front," she said to Haku

In the changing room, the girls slipped on their bathing suits. The one-piece suit fit Rose perfectly and was in one of her favorite shades of blue. Over the suits, they wrapped brightly patterned cloths, then tied them closed. Rose had seen booths selling these pretty cloths—*sarongs*—she had heard someone call them.

The girls jammed their street clothes back into the locker, then headed outside to wait for Haku.

Rose looked around. Everything was so beautiful. The deep blue sky dipped down to touch the distant mountains. Off to her right, the street sloped and ended at the beach. Her legs itched to chase after the shorebirds pecking in the sand, but the warm sun made her feel lazy. Maybe she'd chase the seagulls later.

As they leaned against the cabana, Rose watched the people go by. Some of them rode bikes, and some rushed as though they were late. Most strolled along slowly, stopping to browse or talk to friends. Just looking at them made Rose feel calm and peaceful.

So far, island life suited her just fine.

Haku finally came out of the cabana, his swim trunks actually reaching below his knees! He did look cute, though, Rose thought. And he swaggered as though he were the best surfer on the island. Rose looked away so he wouldn't see her smile. He might think she was laughing at him, and she didn't want to hurt his feelings.

Suddenly Rose's stomach rumbled and she pictured a triple-dip ice cream cone. "Let's go eat. I'm starving!" she suggested.

The three of them wove among the people swarming the streets. As they passed one booth, something caught Rose's attention. She pulled her friends off to the side to listen as a woman spoke in a foreign language and then interpreted it for the onlookers.

"*Ia ora na!*" she said, smiling. "And that is Tahitian for 'Good day!'"

"*Ia ora na!*" Rose repeated, rolling the unfamiliar words off her tongue. It felt a little like when she spoke Cheyenne with her grandfather.

"Let's go," Haku whined.

Rose only half listened to him. Learning another language was so interesting.

"And this is a phrase we like to use on the islands," the woman went on. "'*Aita pe'ape'a!* No problem!"

The crowd laughed as it began to disperse. Rose and Leila walked on until they came to a booth selling all different kinds of ice cream. Out loud, Rose read the handmade sign: "Coconut, guava, pineapple, banana, macadamia nut."

Leila shivered. "Oooh, I don't know which kind to choose."

Stepping up to the counter, Rose turned to ask Haku what he wanted, but he wasn't there. "Where's your brother?" she asked Leila.

Leila turned around. "He's probably off with a friend."

"Haku!" Rose called, but no little boy came running to them.

"Haku!" Leila shouted. When her brother didn't appear, she whirled around, looking through the crowd. "Oh, no, I can't lose him again. Mother will ground me forever."

Rose's pulse picked up speed. Haku was full of himself, but if he really was lost, he was probably scared out of his wits. "Come on, let's find him," she said as she grabbed Leila's hand.

The two girls darted through the crowd, calling Haku's

name. People turned to look at them and moved out of their way.

"Where could he be?" Leila wailed, her voice tinged with both panic and anger.

Rose took her hand. "Don't worry," she said. "I'm sure he's around. Come on." They retraced their steps to the changing rooms.

"You look inside and I'll look around out here," Rose directed.

As Leila dashed into the cabana, Rose circled the building. There were drinking fountains and a couple of showers, but no Haku.

When she saw a group of boys around Haku's age, she ran over to them. "Have you seen a boy in purple and orange shorts?"

"Who are you looking for?" one of the boys asked as he tucked a boogie board under his arm.

"Haku," Rose said. "Uh, I don't know his last name."

The boy and his companions glanced at one another. "Sure, we know Haku," he said. "Saw him just a little while ago." A couple of them giggled, and Rose saw them sneaking glances at a clump of bushes near the cabana.

"We have to go now," the boy said. "Bye." Laughing, the boys ran down the beach.

Something seems a little fishy here, Rose thought, and it has nothing to do with the fish in the ocean.

Leila ran out of the building. "Did you find him?"

Rose grinned at her. "Not yet, but…" Placing her finger over her lips, she tiptoed over to the bushes. When she caught a glimpse of bright orange and purple, she was sure.

With a loud whoop, she lunged into the bushes.

Chapter Five

SURF'S UP!

Haku jumped up with a startled cry from behind the hibiscus bush. "Hey, how did you find me?" he yelped.

"With a little help from your friends," Rose said, laughing at his surprised expression.

"Where were you, Haku?" Leila

demanded with a frown, her hands planted on her hips.

Her brother winced. "I was playing with my friends."
He looked down at his feet and kicked his toe against a
clump of sandy soil. "I didn't think you'd get so worried.
When I heard you calling me I thought you might be mad,
so I hid."

"You hid?" Leila screeched, stepping toward him.

Rose laughed. "Hey, I probably would have done the
same thing."

Leila looked at her friend. Then she smiled. "I guess
you're right." She turned to Haku. "But you have to stop
disappearing on me."

"So you're not mad?" Haku asked hopefully.

"No," Rose said. "But—"

"But? But what?"

Rose grinned at Leila. "But," she continued, "I think
you have to be taught a lesson." She walked toward the
boy with both hands out like Frankenstein's monster.

Haku took a couple of steps backward and bumped
into a water fountain. "I'll never do it again," he promised.

Rose kept clomping forward like a monster, trying not to giggle. "When we get our hands on you…"

Leila joined her. Now there were two stiff-legged creatures after him.

"Sorry, sorry, sorry," Haku said. He looked like he was trying not to giggle.

"We are going to make you suffer…" Leila said in a deep voice.

Haku laughed. "I said I was sorry!"

"And we're not going to stop until you beg for mercy," Rose added.

"What are you going to do to me?" He sounded a little worried now.

"We're going to *tickle* you!" With that, Rose leaped forward, but Haku dodged her and took off running.

Rose and Leila ran down the road to the beach after him, then across the hot sand, sinking a little with each footfall. At last they reached the firmer sand near the water. Just beyond the crashing waves, Haku collapsed, shrieking, even though no one had touched him.

Rose tackled the boy, and sand flew everywhere. She tried to tickle him, but he was wiggling so much it was hard to get her fingers on him.

"I'm sorry! I'm sorry!" he choked out between gasps. "I'll never do it again."

The girls didn't relent. They kept up the tickling until finally all three of them lay in a panting heap.

Rose looked down at herself. She was covered with sticky sand, and it felt like some had crawled into her bathing suit, too. She stood and started to brush off the grit, then turned toward the crashing waves. They were much bigger than any she'd ever seen.

I could jump into the water and wash off, she thought, but those waves look a little too terrifying. It was bad enough to have to surf in them later—if she ever found the nerve to get out there. In the meantime, keeping her feet on dry land seemed like a very good idea.

As the three of them were brushing themselves off, Haku's friends jogged over with their boogie boards. They threw them flat on the edge of the water, then ran and

jumped on, balancing as the thin boards
shot along the shore. The better
ones stayed on until the
boards slowed down,
then jumped off. The
others fell off right away,
usually backward onto their rear
ends with a big splash. Rose winced whenever one of
them hit the waves.

Haku borrowed a board and tossed it onto the water.
He ran, jumped on, and slid smoothly until the board
slowed to a stop.

"It's been a while since I saw Haku on a board," Leila
said. "He does have great balance and good style for an
eight-year-old," she admitted.

Haku took another run, but this time he wobbled and
fell. Clutching his right arm, he gave a loud, sharp cry of
pain. Everyone ran forward.

"Are you hurt?" Leila exclaimed, crouching beside her
brother in the shallow water.

Surf's Up!

Haku squeezed his eyes shut, his mouth pulled back in a grimace. While Rose knelt beside him, she felt the strong undertow sucking at her legs as the water pulled back out to sea.

Suddenly, Haku sat up and waved both arms in the air. Rose didn't even notice that his friends had gathered around them until they started laughing.

Leila jumped to her feet. "That's not funny, Haku!"

Rose frowned. "Someday you're really going to be lost or hurt and no one—" She stopped in midsentence when Haku leaped to his feet and ran off with his giggling friends.

Suddenly Leila squealed and dashed onto the dry sand. Rose stared at her. By the time she looked toward the water to see what had startled her friend, it was too late. A large wave rose and hovered for one second before crashing down on top of her.

Chapter
Six

HEADING FOR DISASTER

The power of the wave smashed Rose to the ground, where she got a big mouthful of sand. Then it swirled her in its undertow.

She felt like a tumbleweed as she rolled this way and that. Frantic for air, she finally pushed against the sandy bottom and shot out of the water, taking a gasping breath. Another surge of water pushed her further onto the shore. Before the undertow could drag her out to sea, Rose clambered up onto drier sand. Then she collapsed.

Leila stood above her. "You looked so surprised!" she said with a giggle. "Didn't you enjoy it?"

Rose groaned silently. Since when were waves fun? She was about to tell Leila she'd had more fun on a broken Ferris wheel, when a tall woman in a red bathing suit, a clipboard in her hand, trotted over to them. "It's almost time," she said.

"For what?" Rose asked.

"For the surfing, of course. Hurry and wax your board and get out there. Watch for the flag to signal the start of the contest." She turned away, and Rose's stomach did a flip-flop.

Rose looked out at the huge waves rolling onto shore one at a time. Now she knew their power firsthand.

"Come on," Leila said, grabbing Rose's hand, "it's time to go for that trophy!"

Obviously her friend wasn't going to let her get out of this. With Leila's help, Rose got to her feet, and on weak legs she walked over to the surfboard stand. It was easy to guess which one was hers. It was hot pink with bright blue waves.

For a moment she watched the other kids. Then she grabbed a hunk of wax and followed their example, rubbing it up and down the board. Haku did the same.

When he was done, Haku picked up his board and headed for the water. "See you after I win!" he called over his shoulder.

Rose wanted to make a comment, but her mouth was too dry to speak.

Leila patted her on the back. "What's the matter?"

Rose shrugged.

"You don't look too well. Do you feel sick?"

"A little," Rose admitted. "I guess I'm kind of nervous."

Leila burst out laughing. "Oh, sure you are—as if the best surfer here could be nervous. You've ridden bigger waves with your eyes closed."

Rose smiled weakly.

"I'll get you some juice," Leila offered. "Maybe you're

just hungry or dehydrated. Thanks to Haku, we missed our snack." Then she ran off.

Rose took deep breaths, trying to calm herself. Just as she finished waxing her board, Leila returned with a cup.

She was out of breath. "All they had was guava, orange or pineapple, so I got you guava."

Rose drank the thick, sour-sweet juice. It tingled her taste buds. After she'd drained the cup, she smiled at her friend. "Thanks. I do feel better now."

"Then you'd better get out there before they start without you."

Rose picked up her surfboard, tucked it under her arm, and walked with Leila to the water's edge. All along the beach, surfers were attaching their ankle leashes. Once again, she did what everyone else was doing. She felt like an ad for the old saying, "Monkey see, monkey do."

After she attached her leash, she watched the others as they lay on their stomachs and paddled out to sea. With a huge lump in her throat, she did the same.

As the first wave approached her head-on, Rose

thought the lump would choke her, but her board slipped up the wave and down the other side. It was exciting—in a scary sort of way!

She had to ride up and down a few waves to get out to where the other surfers were turning their boards in toward shore and waiting to catch a wave.

Rose's mouth still felt dry and she had trouble catching her breath, even though she knew deep down that the mirror wouldn't put her in any real danger. At least she *hoped* it wouldn't…

Once she was in position to catch a wave, Rose gazed at the shore. She was so far out that the people on the beach looked like plastic action figures. Then she glanced behind her. A giant wave rose from the sea, curling its foamy top toward her. She took a deep breath. It was now or never.

She paddled to get her board moving in the same direction as the wave. Then, gripping the sides of the board, she brought her feet up under her. They stuck to the board's surface, and she realized that was what the wax was for. Slowly she stood up, her arms flailing out on either side of her for balance. The water lifted her board and sent her shooting forward.

Rose crouched so she wouldn't tip over. She no longer felt like she might lose her balance. Her arms were still out to the sides, but now they weren't wiggling around like worms on a hook.

Faster and faster, the board practically flew over the water.

After a few moments, Rose discovered that if she leaned to one side, the board shifted direction. She angled it to the side so the wave closed up behind her, but she kept moving forward. Sometimes it even seemed as if she were surfing through a tunnel of water.

At last, close to shore, the wave died out behind her. Slowly, the board lost speed and sank a bit in the water. Rose knelt, then flopped forward onto her belly and turned the board around, heading out again.

As she paddled, she watched the other surfers. Hardly any of them rode a wave all the way in, the way she had.

Some of them fell off about halfway through, the ankle leash keeping their boards near them, and some were knocked off their boards when the big waves swallowed them momentarily. She grinned. Maybe she would win this contest after all.

Rose took a few more warm-up runs, keeping her eye on the flag on shore that would signal the start of the contest. By her fourth wave, she really felt like she had the hang of it. That thought reminded her of a T-shirt her uncle had brought back for her on one of his many vacations. It had the words *Born to Surf* written over a drawing of a wave. She felt she knew what that meant as she leaned back and forth, getting the most out of the wave.

The salty sea spray sprinkled her face, keeping her cool under the hot, tropical sun. This was a blast! How could she ever have been afraid of the ocean? she thought.

Heading for Disaster

Suddenly Rose heard someone shouting. She looked over her shoulder. Immediately her limbs froze in fear.

Haku, crouched on his board, his face filled with terror, was heading right for her!

Chapter
Seven

ROSE TO THE RESCUE

Rose only had a second to decide her next move. She jumped off her board. When she surfaced, she wiped the salt from her eyes and saw that Haku's surfboard was coming at her like a torpedo.

He raised his head and stared at her. Was that a grin on his face?

Sudden anger burned through Rose. Haku could have

caused a dangerous accident with his fooling around. First he'd taken off without telling them, then he'd faked hurting his arm, and now this. Why did he have to be such a show-off?

Rose climbed on her board to catch the next wave, her gaze fixed on Haku as he doubled over and dropped to his knees, clutching his stomach.

She clenched her fists. Was he faking this, too? Probably, she thought to herself, being the joker he was. But a little wiggle of doubt swam around inside her like a goldfish in a small bowl.

Haku still had his arms wrapped around his middle. Suddenly the wave tipped his board over and he splashed into the sea. The board flipped once, twice, three times, then floated on the water.

Rose strained her eyes, watching for the boy to surface. She knew he was wearing his ankle leash, so he had to be close to his board. But where? And why didn't he come up for air?

Now her stomach churned with real fear. Even playing

a joke, he couldn't stay underwater that long, could he?

Rose aimed her board toward his and paddled quickly over to it. Haku still hadn't appeared. Just then a waving flag on the shore caught her attention. The contest was beginning. If she didn't start surfing now, there was no way she could win. But where was Haku?

She looked around frantically for the boy. It seemed like long minutes had ticked by, although she knew it had only been seconds. She grabbed Haku's board, then reached for the leash and gripped it tight, pulling it toward her. At last her hand touched a foot. Using all her strength, she hoisted Haku onto his board so he lay across it on his stomach, his head resting at the top. Immediately he coughed up big mouthfuls of seawater.

Rose pushed on his back, trying to force out more of the water.

Suddenly he lifted his head, coughing and sputtering. Worried that there might be more water caught in his lungs, Rose started to swim toward shore, dragging Haku and the two boards with her.

The huge waves rolling in behind her helped, but still she could feel the fierce undertow trying to pull them back out to sea. And, little waves kept slapping her in the face, filling her mouth, nose, and eyes with salty, stinging water.

Rose's heart hammered in her chest like ancient island drums. She didn't even notice all the people swimming out to help till she got close to shore.

Leila was one of the first to reach her. "We didn't see

what happened. Are you okay?" she asked frantically.

Rose nodded, too exhausted to answer. Her limbs felt like chunks of waterlogged wood. At the water's edge, she fumbled with her ankle strap. Finally she released it and tried to tug her board onto the sand. It suddenly weighed ten tons. Gratefully she let Leila bring it ashore for her while she collapsed on the sand.

Rose looked up to see a paramedic crouching over Haku, checking his pulse and breathing and other vital signs. After a few moments, he announced that the boy would be fine.

The crowd dispersed, their attention back on the surfing contest.

Haku sat up, a hand on his stomach. "I'm sorry I messed up the contest for you."

"What happened out there?" Rose asked, panting weakly.

"I got a stomach cramp."

"I thought you were aiming at me on purpose," Rose admitted. "That you were fooling around again."

Haku's cheeks had turned red. "Uh, actually"—he took a deep breath— "actually I *was* fooling around at first. I was going to pretend to be out of control to scare you for fun."

"Are you crazy?" his sister demanded. "You could have hurt Rose. Don't you know any better?"

He hung his head and dug his toes into the sand.

Leila sighed. "Haku, you've just *got* to think about what you're doing." She leaned down and gave him a little hug, her flash of anger gone.

Rose stood, still feeling totally waterlogged. "Well, I guess it's too late for me to join the contest now." She tried not to sound as relieved as she felt. "I think I'll go back and change into my clothes."

"Don't you want to stay and watch the other surfers?" Leila asked.

Rose smiled and shook her head.

Leila and Haku stood up. Leila hugged her. "See you later."

Haku hugged her, too. "Do you forgive me?"

Rose nodded. "Of course I do. Only from now on, don't

get in so much trouble."

"Don't worry. And thanks for saving me."

Rose grinned. "'*Aita pe'ape'a*! No problem!"

Leila and Haku smiled.

Rose took a deep breath, smelling the wonderful salt and perfume of the flowers in the breeze. She took one last look at the palms along the beautiful shoreline. Island living was great, but she had something important to do.

With a wave to her friends, she turned and jogged back to the changing rooms. She put on the shorts and top and grass skirt she had arrived in, and stepped into her sandals. Then she walked over to the wall mirror and smiled at her reflection.

Chapter

Eight

THE SOUND OF MUSIC

T he next thing Rose knew, she was back in Ellie's cozy attic. She quickly changed into her clothes and rushed downstairs.

Piano sounds still came from the music room. Good, she wasn't too late.

Just then the doorbell rang. Rose didn't know whether it would be polite for her to answer the door, so she waited, hoping it wasn't Mrs. Muller coming to pick up Blake. She had to talk to him first.

Ellie came out of the music room and smiled at Rose. "We're almost done, dear." She opened the front door.

Heather, Keisha, Alison, and Megan were standing there, peering in through the doorway.

"We came by to say hi," Alison said.

Rose shook her head. She knew they wanted to know if she'd talked to Ellie about her Bratty Blake problem.

"Come on in," Ellie offered, moving out of the way. "It's always such a delight to see you all. I'm just finishing up a lesson."

The girls crowded into the foyer as Ellie headed back to the music room.

"Uh, could we listen to Blake sing?" Rose blurted out before she changed her mind.

The girls stared at her as if she were crazy.

Rose smiled at Ellie, ignoring her friends. "Blake is always telling me what a great singer he is, and I'd like to hear him."

Just then the boy appeared at the music room door and grinned at Rose. "Sure," he said. "You can come listen to me."

They all filed into the room and sat down on chairs that were set up for recitals. Rose's friends nudged her questioningly, but she put her finger to her lips. She'd explain everything later.

Blake stood beside the grand piano. As Ellie settled

herself before the ivory keys, he said in a formal voice, "I will now sing a song to you from *The Sound of Music*. This is a song about a little white flower."

When Ellie was ready, he nodded to her, and she began to play.

As he sang, he lifted his chin and smiled. His voice, perfect in pitch and tone, filled the room, lilting and dancing like colorful butterflies through the Swiss Alps.

When he finished and bowed to his audience, Rose and the other girls burst into applause.

Blake grinned at them. "Did you really like it?"

Rose stood up, still clapping. "You were great. Honest!"

Blake's face turned pink. "You're not just saying that?"

"No way. You really were fantastic!"

"I wish I could sing as well as you do," Keisha said wistfully.

"You could if you practiced," Blake said with a grin. "Lots and lots of practice."

Just at that moment, Mrs. Muller arrived to take her son home.

Rose told her she'd be at their house the following Thursday for another computer lesson. "But only if you promise to sing me another song," she said to Blake.

Blake's smiled stretched from ear to ear. "I promise!"

After Blake and his mother had left, Ellie turned to her. "Rose, what was it you wanted to talk to me about?"

"Oh, it wasn't anything important, and I've kind of worked it out by myself."

"That's wonderful, dear," Ellie said with a smile. "It always feels so good to solve your own problems, doesn't it?"

The girls nodded.

"Now I have a favor to ask of you all," Ellie said, leading them into the kitchen. "I've invented a new kind of dessert, and I really need some expert opinions on it before I serve it to the Arts Council. Would you all taste-test it for me?"

Rose grinned at her friends and licked her lips. She loved doing these kinds of favors for Ellie.

Teasingly, Megan said, "That depends on the ingredients."

Ellie's eyes sparkled like a blue ocean. "Let's see, there are strawberries and chocolate in it, and cream and sugar, a bit of butter too, and—"

"Sounds good to me," Rose said, rubbing her stomach. "I'll be your taste-tester any day!"

Diary

Dear Diary,

Blake is such a neat kid. I never thought I'd say that about him, but it's true. Once I figured out that he just wanted some extra attention, he's acted like an angel and stopped bragging about how great he is.

I told him I'd only listen if he paid attention when I taught him about the computer. It worked! Now he sings a song for me after each lesson.

I can't believe how much he's learned about computers in the last few weeks. In fact, if he ever loses his voice, he'll make a terrific computer programmer.

I saw Ellie yesterday. She complained that all Blake talks about is his computer lessons and how great he is on the computer. I burst

out laughing. Ellie must have known what was
going on, because she laughed, too.

I'll write again soon.

Rose